Disney's POCAHONTAS

Illustrated by the Disney Storybook Artists
Story adapted by Amy Adair

© Disney Enterprises, Inc.

Published by
Louis Weber, C.E.O.
Publications International, Ltd.
7373 North Cicero Avenue
Lincolnwood, Illinois 60712

www.pilbooks.com

Manufactured in China.

8 7 6 5 4 3 2 1

ISBN: 0-7853-9772-8

Long long ago a ship set sail. John Smith and his crew were headed to a new land. John Smith loved to have adventures. He was very brave and strong.

Across the sea, Pocahontas explored the land with her friends Meeko the raccoon and Flit the hummingbird. Pocahontas was also very brave. She stood on the edge of a cliff and soaked in all the beauty that surrounded her.

"Come down!" yelled Pocahontas's friend Nakoma.

Pocahontas dove off the cliff and splashed into the cool water. She climbed into her friend's canoe.

"I've been thinking about that dream again," said Pocahontas. "I think I'll ask my father about it."

John Smith saved Powhatan's life! But he was hurt very badly by Ratcliffe's shot. The settlers were very angry at Ratcliffe. They tied him up and took him back to the ship.

John Smith needed a doctor's help. He had to go back to England. He was very sad. He did not want to leave Pocahontas or the beautiful New World.

Pocahontas and her tribe brought blankets and food to the ship's crew for the voyage.

"You are always welcome here," Powhatan told John Smith, covering him with his own cloak. The chief thanked him for saving his life.

Pocahontas ran through the forest. She arrived in the village just in time. Her father was angrily towering over John Smith.

Pocahontas threw herself on John Smith. "This is where the path of hatred has brought us!" Pocahontas cried.

Powhatan's heart changed. He knew his daughter was right. He also wanted peace, and he dropped his weapon.

Everyone else dropped their weapons, too. But a settler named Ratcliffe still wanted to fight. He aimed his rifle at Powhatan. John Smith jumped in front of Powhatan, knocking him out of the way.

Pocahontas sat sadly with Meeko, Flit, and Percy the dog. She did not think she could stop her father from fighting with the settlers.

"I was wrong," Pocahontas cried. "I must have followed the wrong path."

Just then, Meeko handed Pocahontas the compass that belonged to John Smith. The arrow was spinning round and round. Pocahontas realized the compass arrow was the same arrow from her dream!

"John Smith is my path!" Pocahontas exclaimed. She ran as fast as she could to the village.

That night, Pocahontas slipped out of her village. Nakoma thought her friend was in trouble, so she told Kocoum to follow her.

John Smith and Pocahontas met again. They wished the warriors and the settlers could be friends. They knew they could teach each other many things.

"You have to come with me and talk to my father," Pocahontas said. Suddenly, Kocoum jumped out of the trees. John Smith's friend, Thomas, was hiding in the brush. He thought his friend was in trouble, so he fired a shot at Kocoum! The great warrior fell to the ground.

Thomas ran away. The other warriors captured John Smith and took him back to their village.

"I want to show you something," Pocahontas said.

She led John Smith deep into the forest. She showed him all the beautiful rivers, plants, and animals that called the forest home. John Smith had never appreciated nature's true beauty before.

Boom! Boom! Boom! Drums suddenly sounded in the distance. "The drums mean there is trouble!" Pocahontas said with alarm.

Pocahontas and John Smith couldn't wait to see each other again. Finally, they were able to meet up at the river and talk.

"We will show your people how to use this land properly," John Smith explained.

Pocahontas was upset by what he said. It was her people that knew the land and believed that every thing had a spirit.

Pocahontas started to run away.

"No, wait please!" Smith called after her.

Pocahontas was scared. But she remembered that Grandmother Willow had told her to listen to her heart, so she stopped.

"Who are you?" John Smith asked.

"Pocahontas," she replied.

But Powhatan's warriors had seen John Smith's ship too. The warriors wanted to find out more about the strangers, so they went to spy on them.

Woof! A dog barked at one of the warriors hidden in the trees. It scared the settlers.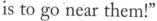

Bang! A shot went off. One of the warriors was wounded in the leg.

Powhatan examined the strange wound. "We will fight this enemy!" Powhatan said. "They are dangerous. No one is to go near them!"

But the clouds were really a ship. John Smith climbed off his ship and explored the new land. He felt someone watching him. Smith jumped through a waterfall toward the stranger. He came face to face with Pocahontas.

"The spinning arrow is pointing you down your path,"
said Grandmother Willow.

"But what is my path?" Pocahontas asked.

"Listen to your heart," Grandmother Willow said
wisely, "and it will guide you."

Suddenly a cool breeze whistled through the leaves.
Pocahontas saw strange white clouds floating across the sea.

Pocahontas was confused. She wanted her father to be happy, but she also wanted to follow her dream. She visited Grandmother Willow and told her all about the strange dream.

"I'm running through the woods," Pocahontas explained, "when I see an arrow in front of me. It spins faster and faster, until it suddenly stops."

When Pocahontas returned to her village, she tried to tell her father, Chief Powhatan, about her dream.

"Father," Pocahontas started, "I had a very strange dream. I think it is telling me that something exciting is about to happen."

"Something exciting *is* about to happen," Powhatan said. "Kocoum has asked to seek your hand in marriage."

"Marry Kocoum?" said Pocahontas. Kocoum was very serious. He did not like to explore like Pocahontas did. "But I think my dream is pointing me down another path," said Pocahontas.

"You are the daughter of the chief," Powhatan said. "It's time to take your place among our people. Even the wild mountain stream must someday join the big river."